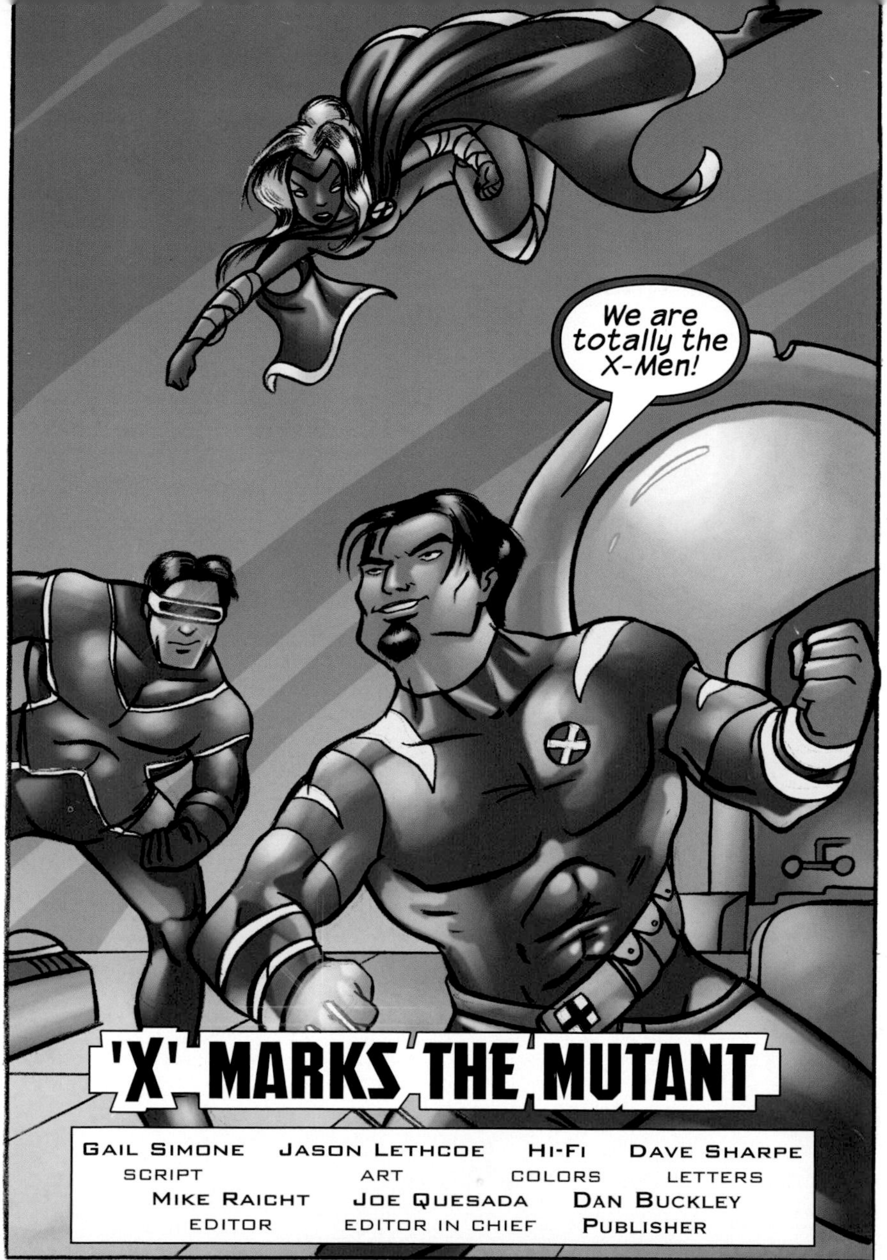
We are totally the X-Men!
'X' MARKS THE MUTANT
GAIL SIMONE SCRIPT
JASON LETHCOE ART
HI-FI COLORS
DAVE SHARPE LETTERS
MIKE RAICHT EDITOR
JOE QUESADA EDITOR IN CHIEF
DAN BUCKLEY PUBLISHER

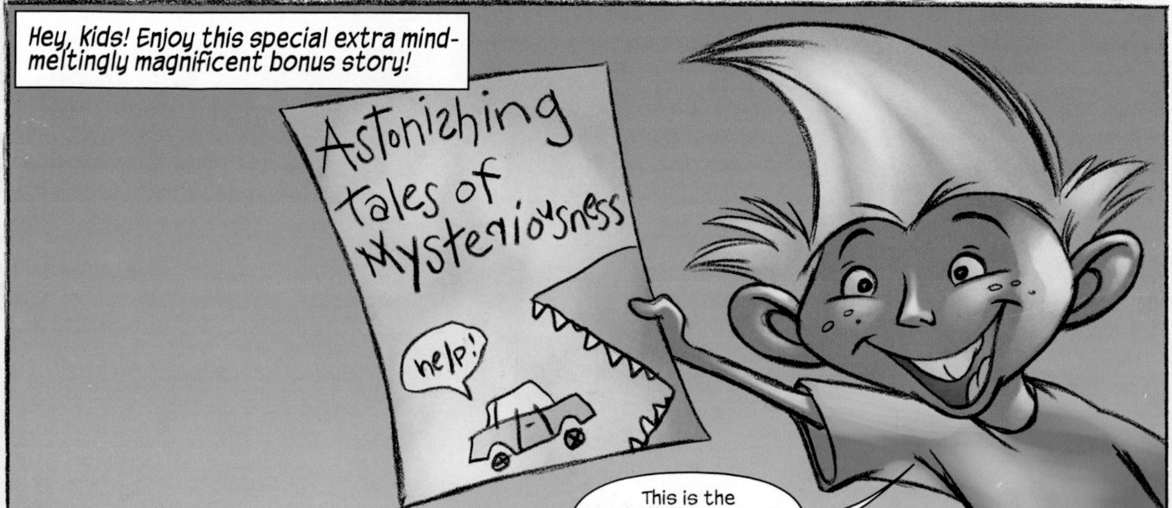
Hey, kids! Enjoy this special extra mind-meltingly magnificent bonus story!
Astonizhing tales of Mysteriousness
help!
This is the story of the fantastic *movie* I'm gonna make someday!

VISIT US AT
www.abdopublishing.com

Spotlight, a division of ABDO Publishing Company Inc., is the school and library distributor of the Marvel Entertainment books.

Library bound edition © 2006

Library of Congress Cataloging-in-Publication Data

Simone, Gail.
    "X" marks the mutant / Gail Simone, script ; Jason Lethcoe, art ; Hi-Fi, colors ; Dave Sharpe, letters. -- Library bound ed.
        p. cm. -- (The marvelous adventures of Gus Beezer series)
    Cover title: Marvelous adventures of Gus Beezer with the X-men
    "Marvel age"--Cover.
    Revision of the May 2003 issue of X-Men.
    ISBN-13: 978-1-59961-050-4
    ISBN-10: 1-59961-050-7
    1. Graphic novels. I. Lethcoe, Jason. II. X-men (New York, N.Y. : 1995). III. Title. IV. Title: Marvelous adventures of Gus Beezer with the X-men. V. Series.

PN6728.X2S57 2006
741.5'973--dc22

                                                          2006043969

All Spotlight books are reinforced library binding and manufactured in the United States of America.

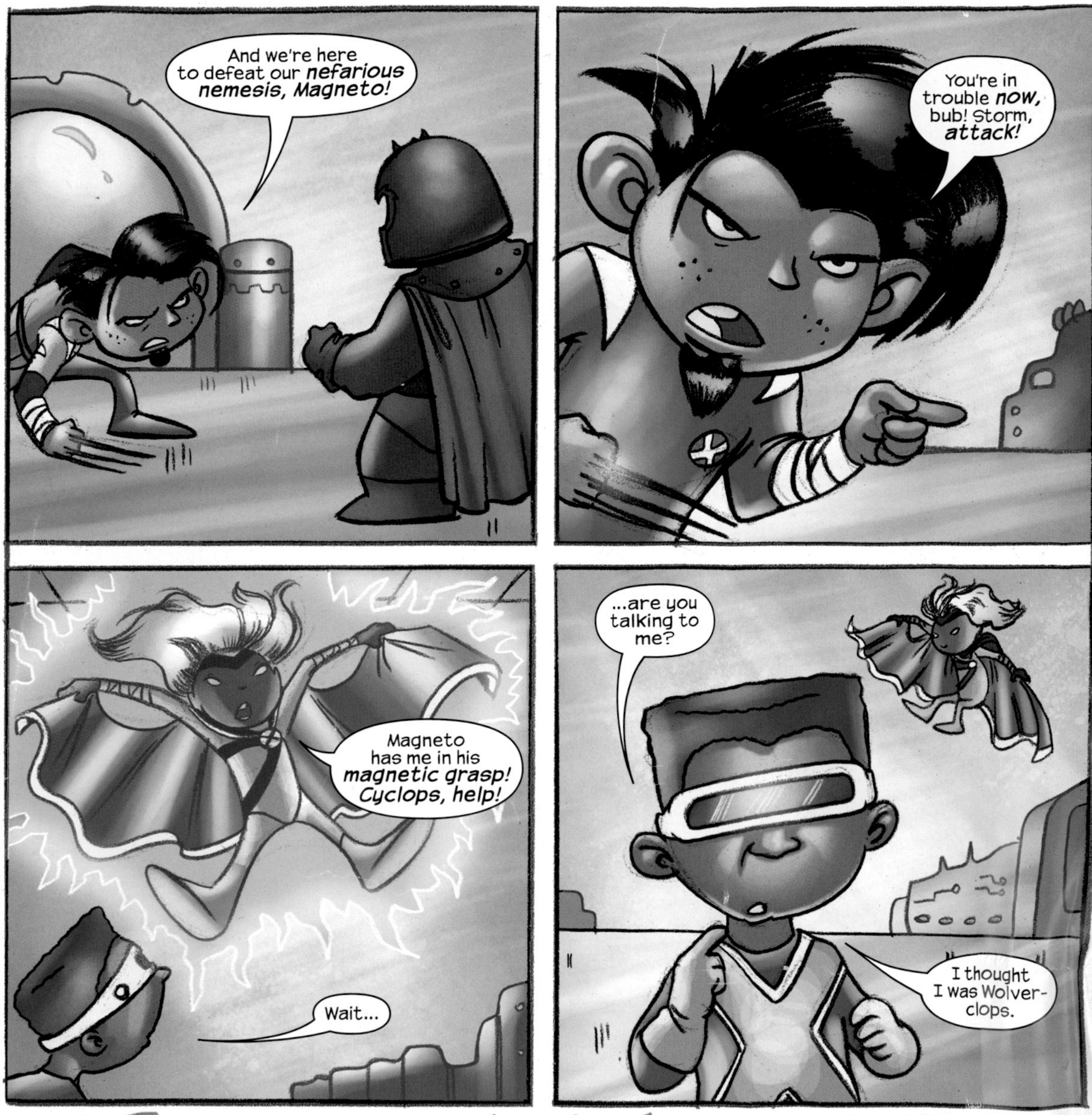
And we're here to defeat our nefarious nemesis, Magneto!
You're in trouble now, bub! Storm, attack!
Magneto has me in his magnetic grasp! Cyclops, help!
Wait...
...are you talking to me?
I thought I was Wolver-clops.

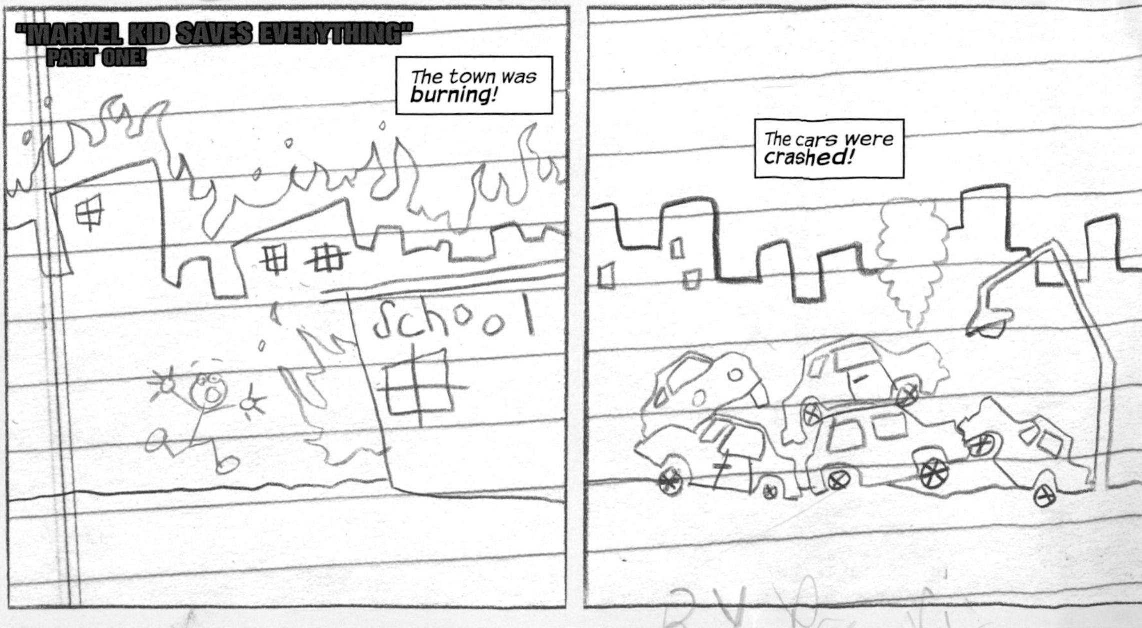
"MARVEL KID SAVES EVERYTHING"
PART ONE!
The town was burning!
School
The cars were crashed!

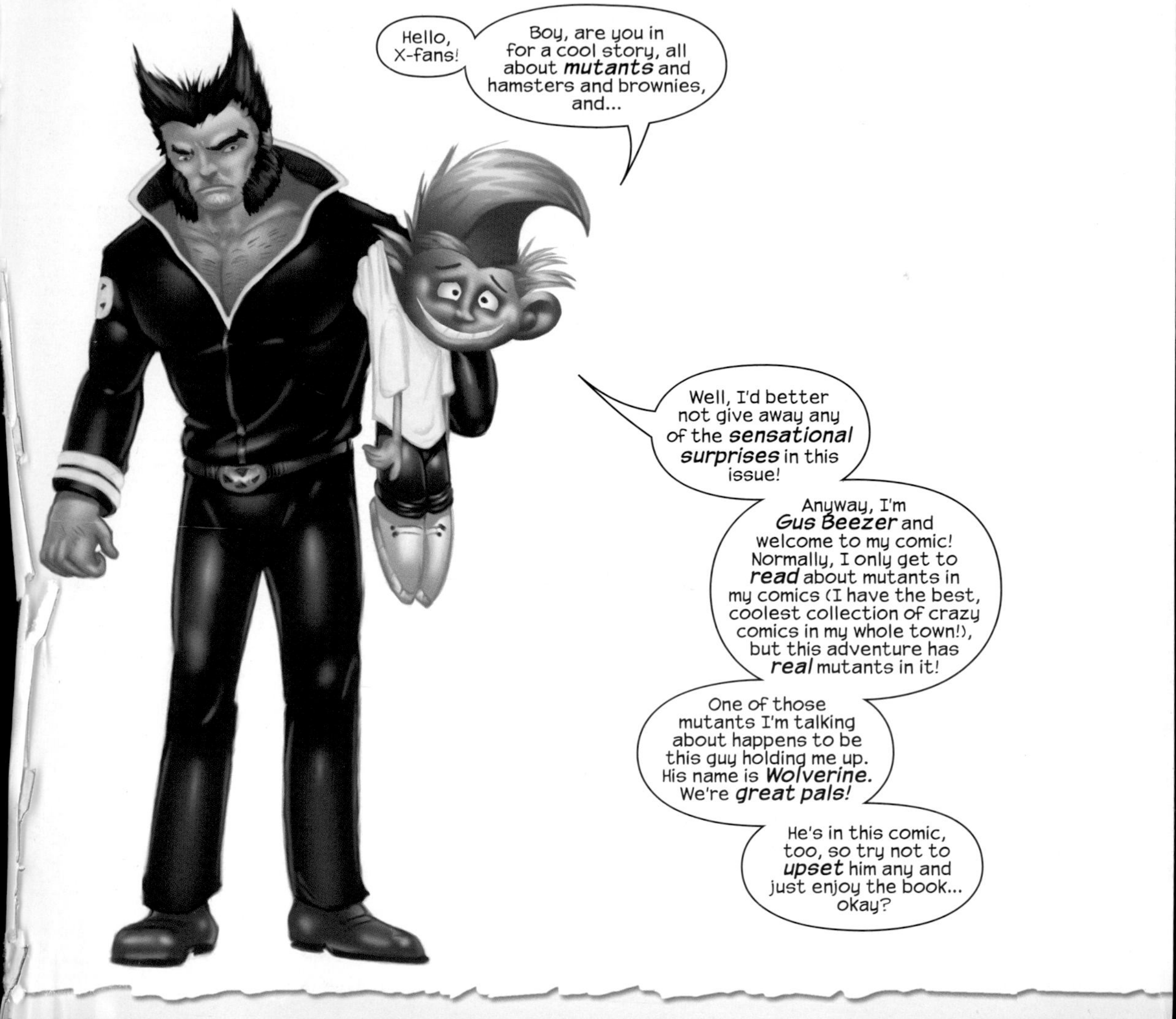
Hello, X-fans!
Boy, are you in for a cool story, all about *mutants* and hamsters and brownies, and...
Well, I'd better not give away any of the *sensational surprises* in this issue!
Anyway, I'm *Gus Beezer* and welcome to my comic! Normally, I only get to *read* about mutants in my comics (I have the best, coolest collection of crazy comics in my whole town!), but this adventure has *real* mutants in it!
One of those mutants I'm talking about happens to be this guy holding me up. His name is *Wolverine.* We're *great pals!*
He's in this comic, too, so try not to *upset* him any and just enjoy the book... okay?
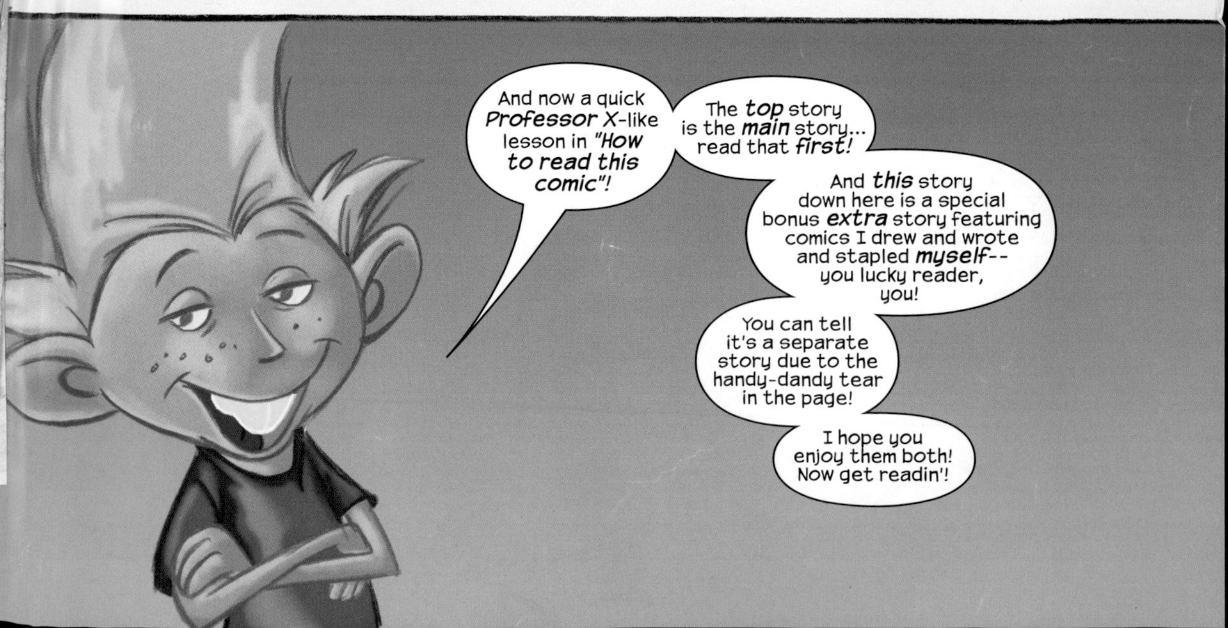
And now a quick *Professor X*-like lesson in *"How to read this comic"*!
The *top* story is the *main* story... read that *first!*
And *this* story down here is a special bonus *extra* story featuring comics I drew and wrote and stapled *myself*-- you lucky reader, you!
You can tell it's a separate story due to the handy-dandy tear in the page!
I hope you enjoy them both! Now get readin'!

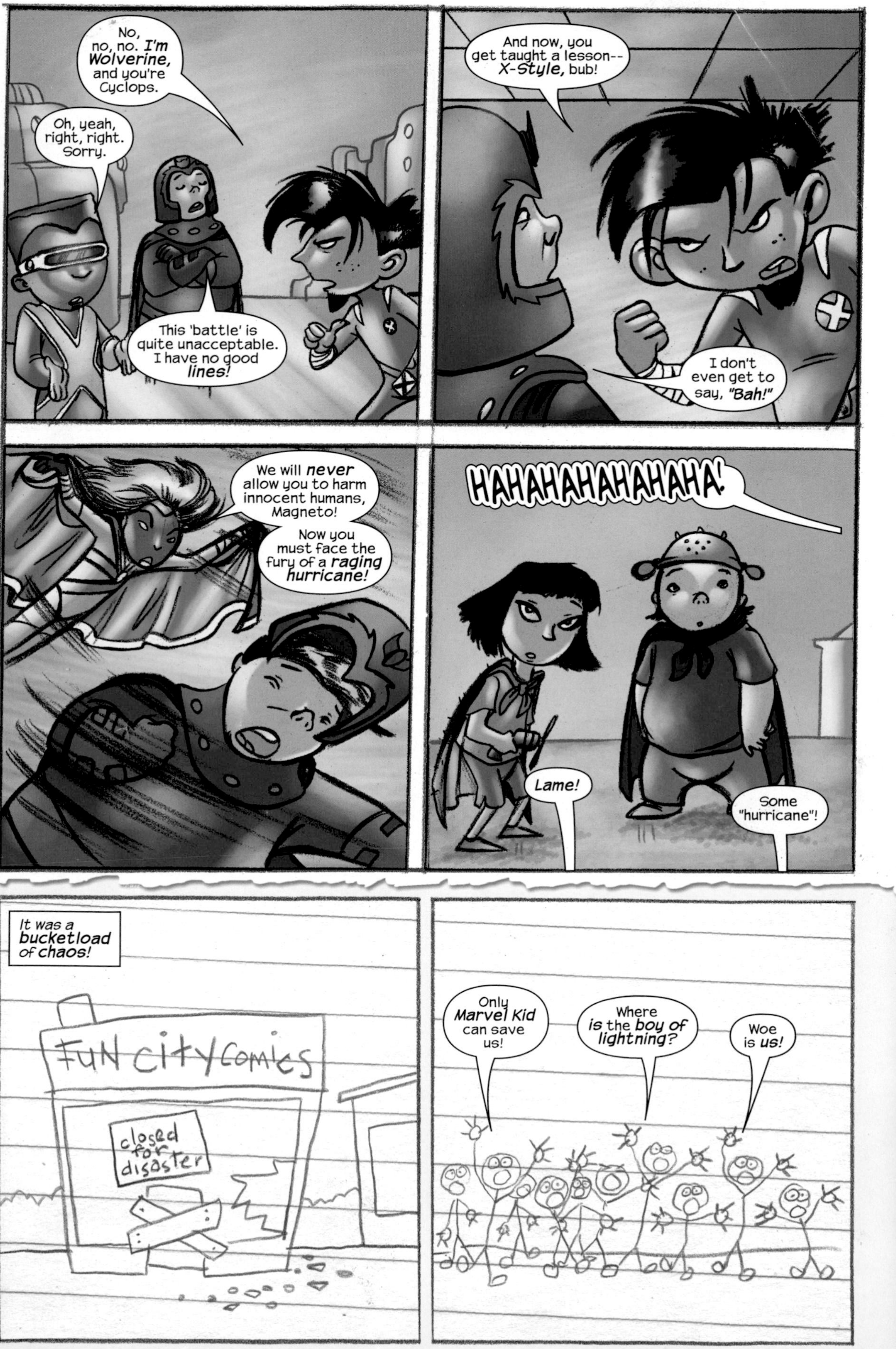

No, no, no. I'm Wolverine, and you're Cyclops.
Oh, yeah, right, right. Sorry.
This 'battle' is quite unacceptable. I have no good lines!
And now, you get taught a lesson-- X-Style, bub!
I don't even get to say, "Bah!"
We will never allow you to harm innocent humans, Magneto!
Now you must face the fury of a raging hurricane!
HAHAHAHAHAHAHA!
Lame!
Some "hurricane"!
It was a bucketload of chaos!
FuN city comics
closed for disaster
Only Marvel Kid can save us!
Where is the boy of lightning?
Woe is us!

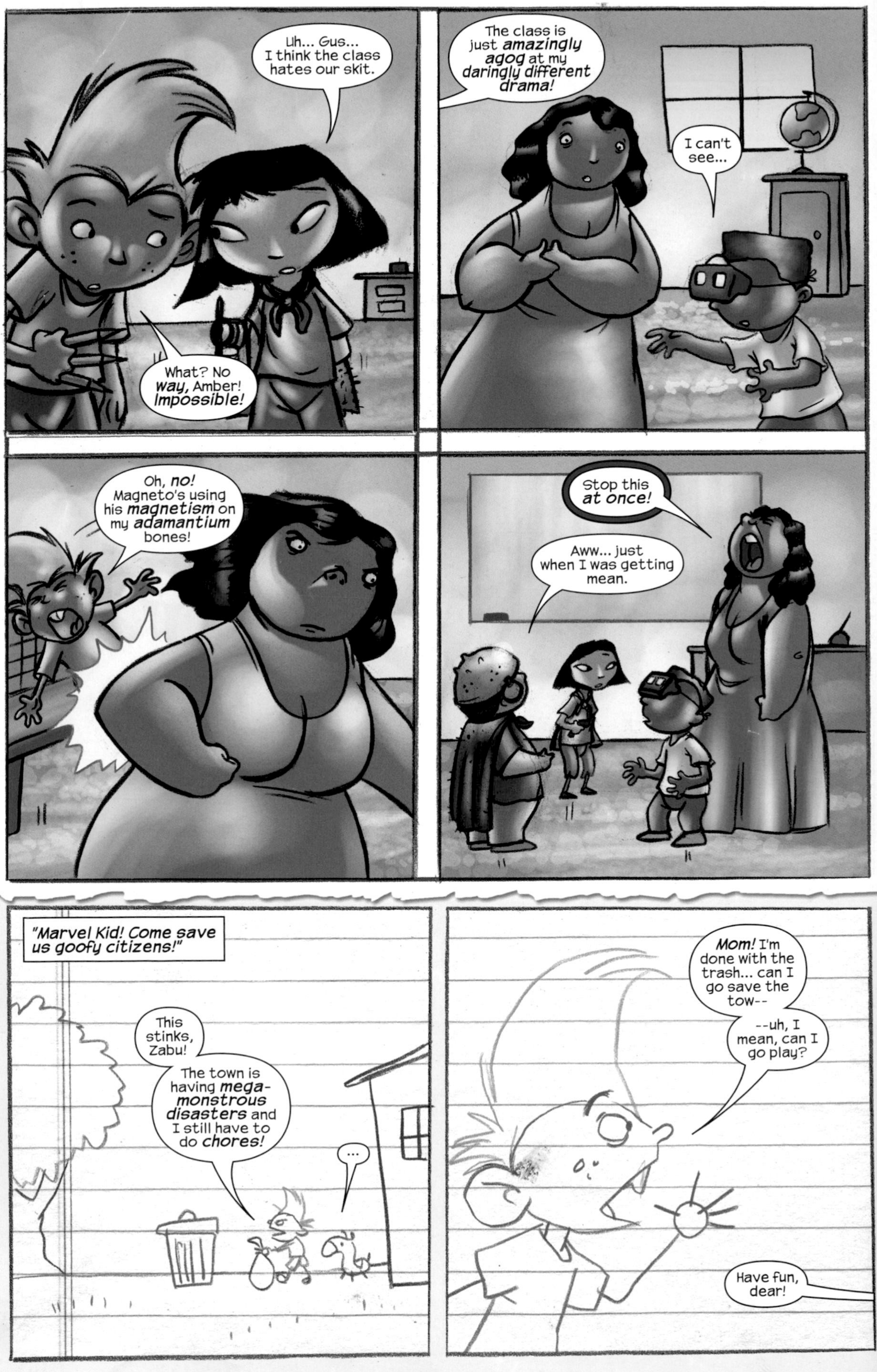

Uh... Gus... I think the class hates our skit.
What? No way, Amber! Impossible!
The class is just amazingly agog at my daringly different drama!
I can't see...
Oh, no! Magneto's using his magnetism on my adamantium bones!
Stop this at once!
Aww... just when I was getting mean.
"Marvel Kid! Come save us goofy citizens!"
This stinks, Zabu!
The town is having mega-monstrous disasters and I still have to do chores!
...
Mom! I'm done with the trash... can I go save the tow--
--uh, I mean, can I go play?
Have fun, dear!

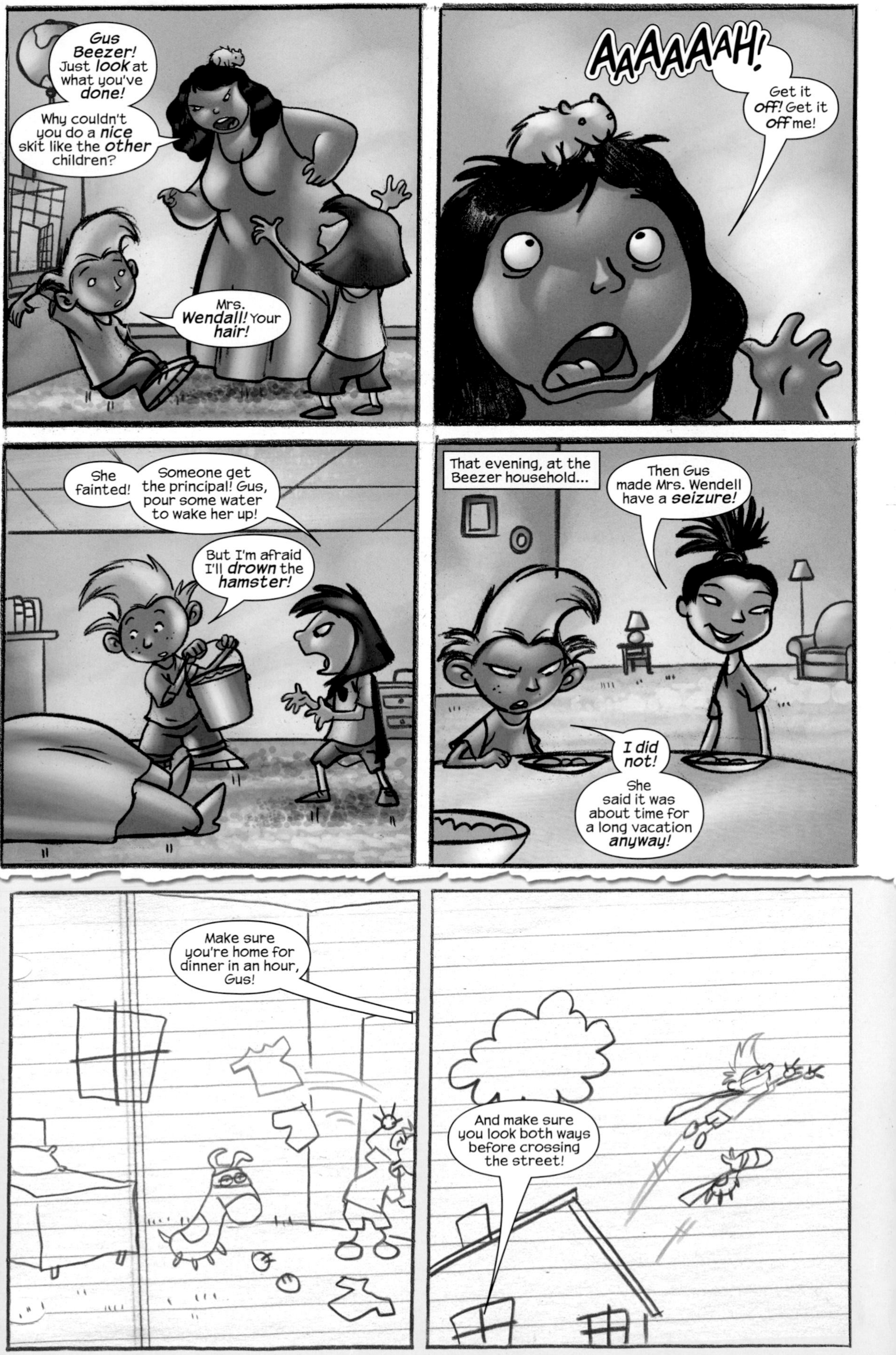
Gus Beezer! Just look at what you've done!
Why couldn't you do a nice skit like the other children?
Mrs. Wendall! Your hair!
AAAAAAH!
Get it off! Get it off me!
She fainted!
Someone get the principal! Gus, pour some water to wake her up!
But I'm afraid I'll drown the hamster!
That evening, at the Beezer household...
Then Gus made Mrs. Wendell have a seizure!
I did not!
She said it was about time for a long vacation anyway!
Make sure you're home for dinner in an hour, Gus!
And make sure you look both ways before crossing the street!

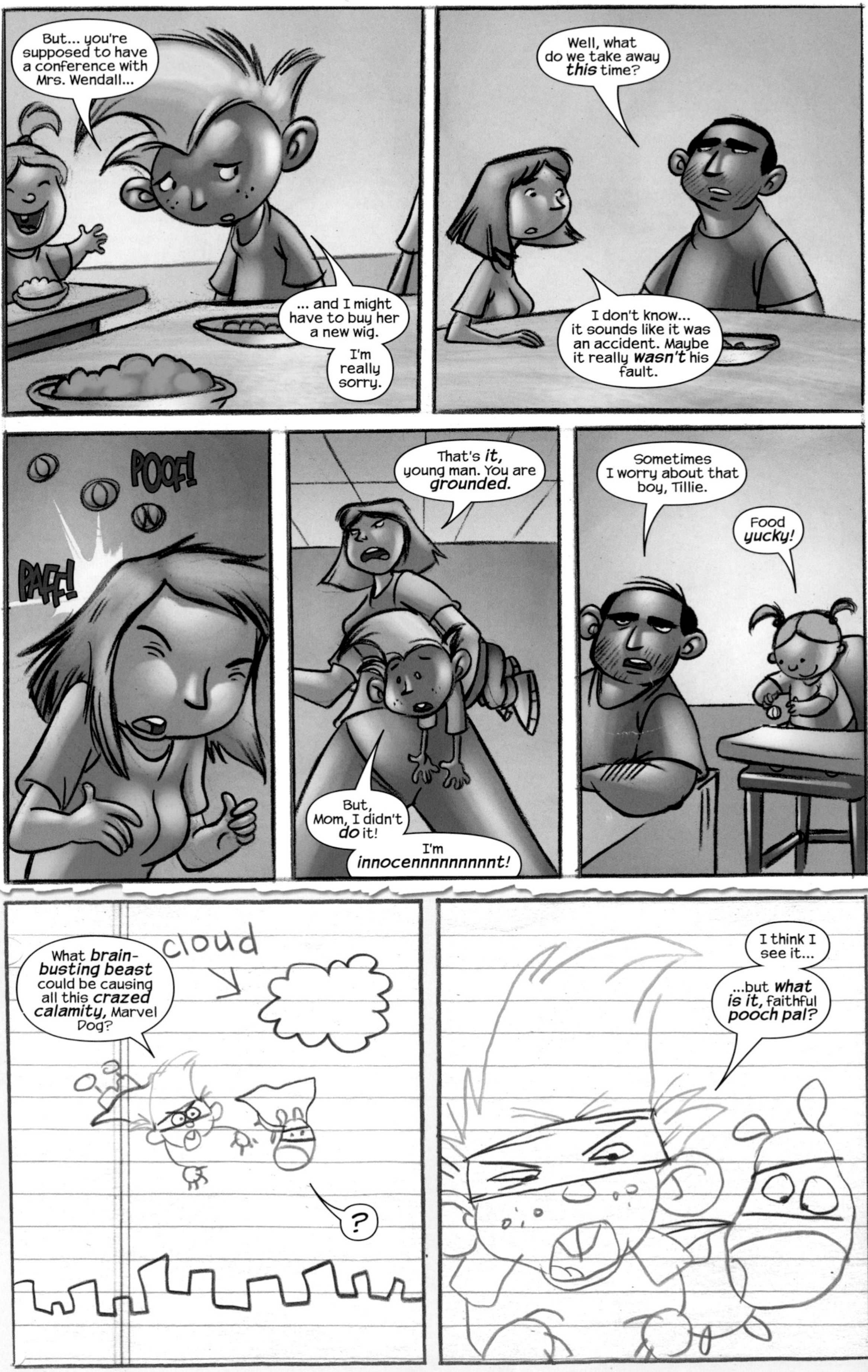

But... you're supposed to have a conference with Mrs. Wendall...
... and I might have to buy her a new wig.
I'm really sorry.
Well, what do we take away *this* time?
I don't know... it sounds like it was an accident. Maybe it really *wasn't* his fault.
POOF!
PAFF!
That's *it*, young man. You are *grounded.*
But, Mom, I didn't *do* it!
I'm *innocennnnnnnnnt!*
Sometimes I worry about that boy, Tillie.
Food *yucky!*
What *brain-busting beast* could be causing all this *crazed calamity,* Marvel Dog?
cloud
?
I think I see it...
...but *what is it,* faithful *pooch pal?*

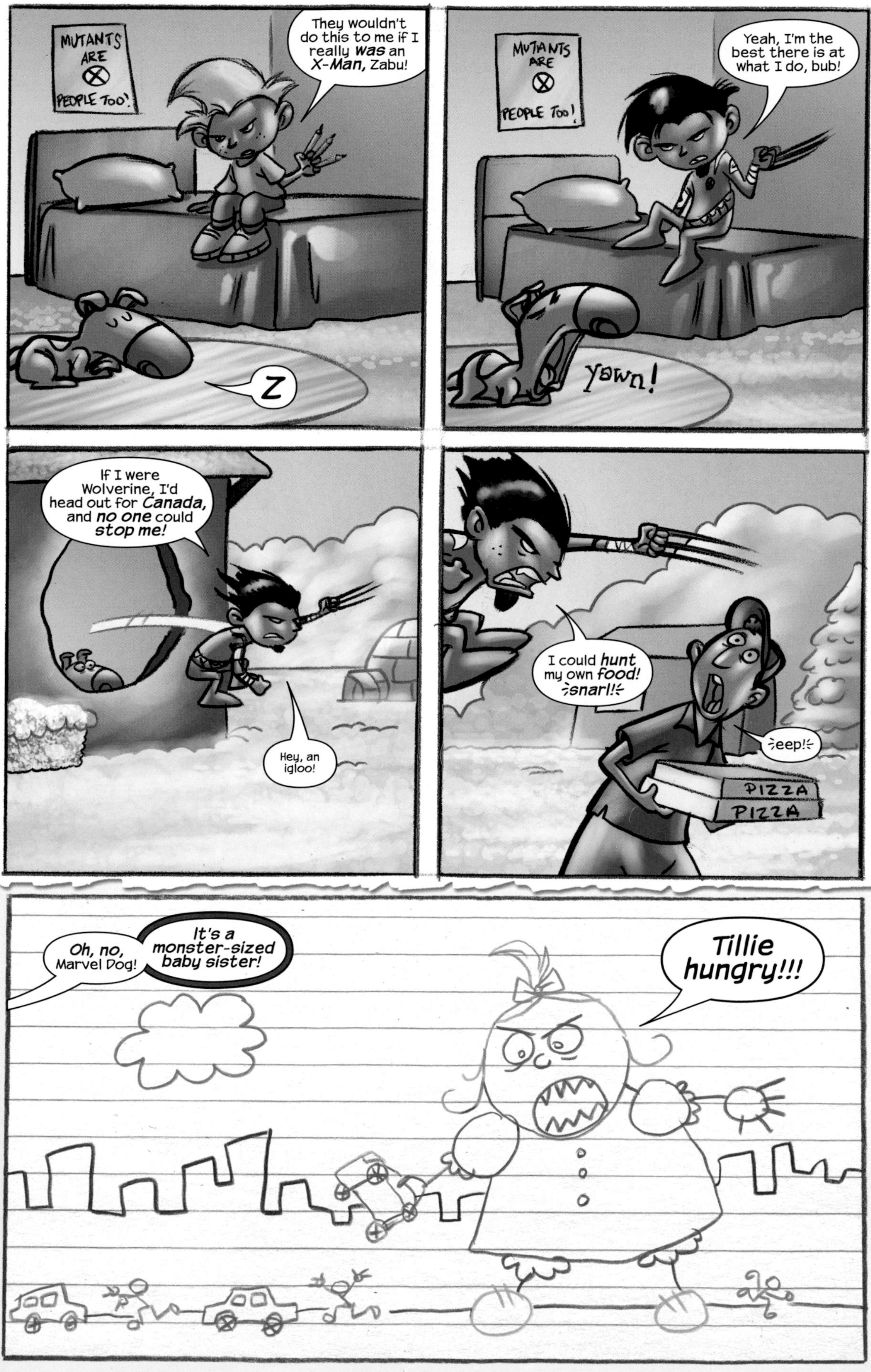
MUTANTS ARE PEOPLE TOO!
They wouldn't do this to me if I really *was* an *X-Man,* Zabu!
Z
MUTANTS ARE PEOPLE TOO!
Yeah, I'm the best there is at what I do, bub!
yawn!
If I were Wolverine, I'd head out for *Canada,* and *no one* could *stop me!*
Hey, an igloo!
I could *hunt* my own *food!* snarl!
eep!
PIZZA
PIZZA
Oh, no, Marvel Dog!
It's a monster-sized baby sister!
Tillie hungry!!!

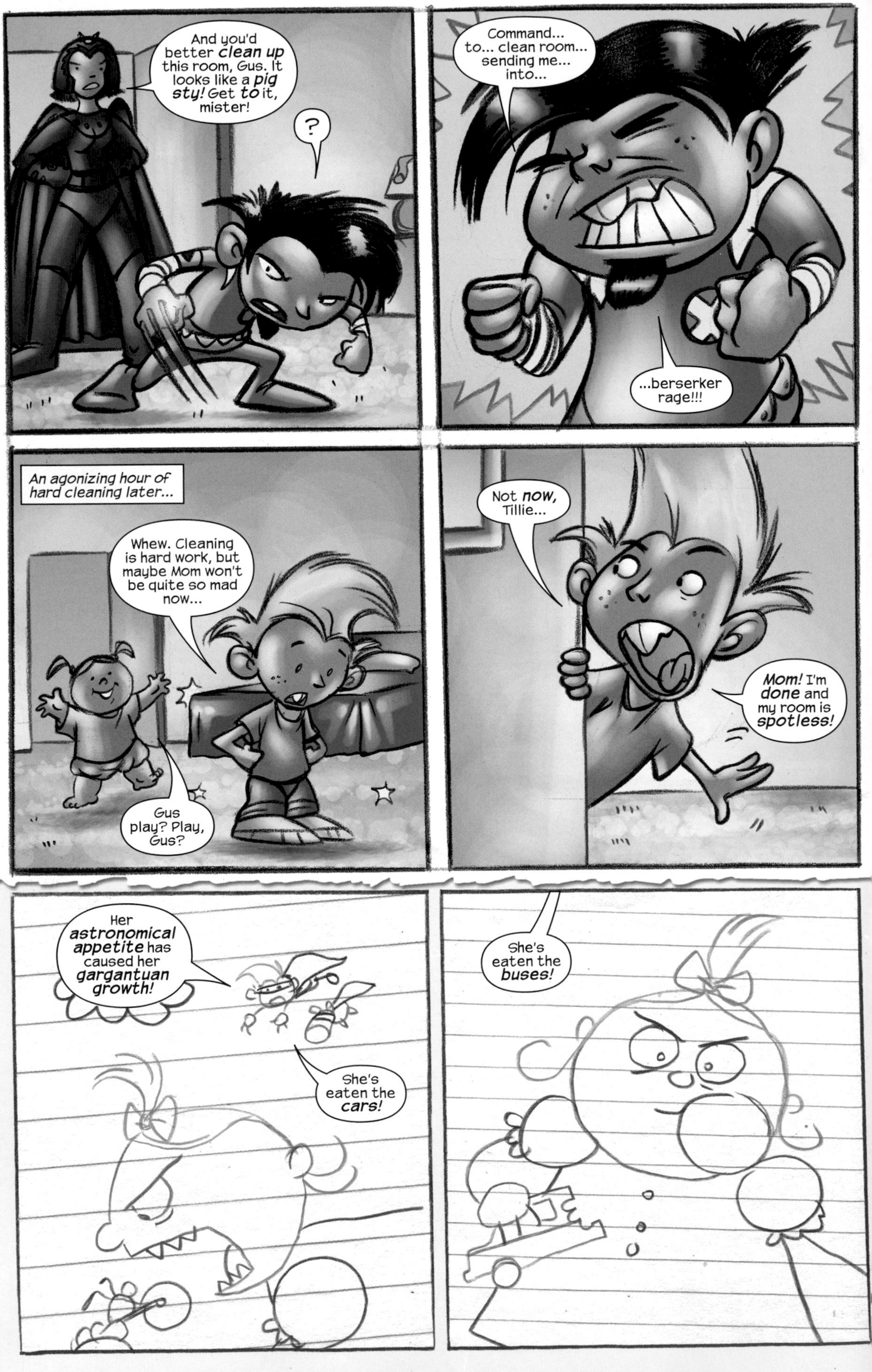

And you'd better clean up this room, Gus. It looks like a pig sty! Get to it, mister!
?
Command... to... clean room... sending me... into...
...berserker rage!!!
An agonizing hour of hard cleaning later...
Whew. Cleaning is hard work, but maybe Mom won't be quite so mad now...
Gus play? Play, Gus?
Not now, Tillie...
Mom! I'm done and my room is spotless!
Her astronomical appetite has caused her gargantuan growth!
She's eaten the cars!
She's eaten the buses!

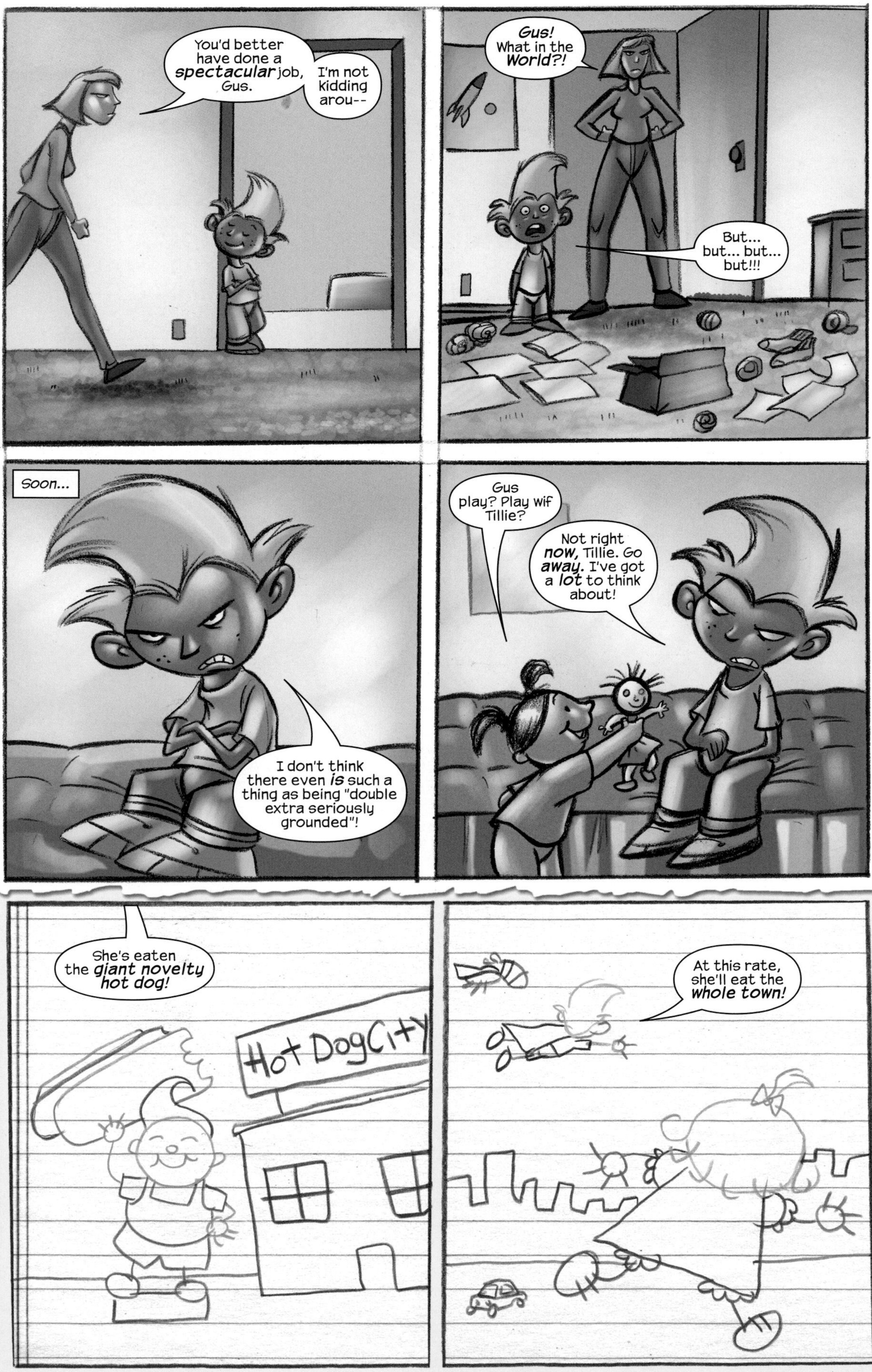
You'd better have done a spectacular job, Gus.
I'm not kidding arou--
Gus! What in the World?!
But... but... but... but!!!
Soon...
I don't think there even is such a thing as being "double extra seriously grounded"!
Gus play? Play wif Tillie?
Not right now, Tillie. Go away. I've got a lot to think about!
She's eaten the giant novelty hot dog!
Hot Dog City
At this rate, she'll eat the whole town!

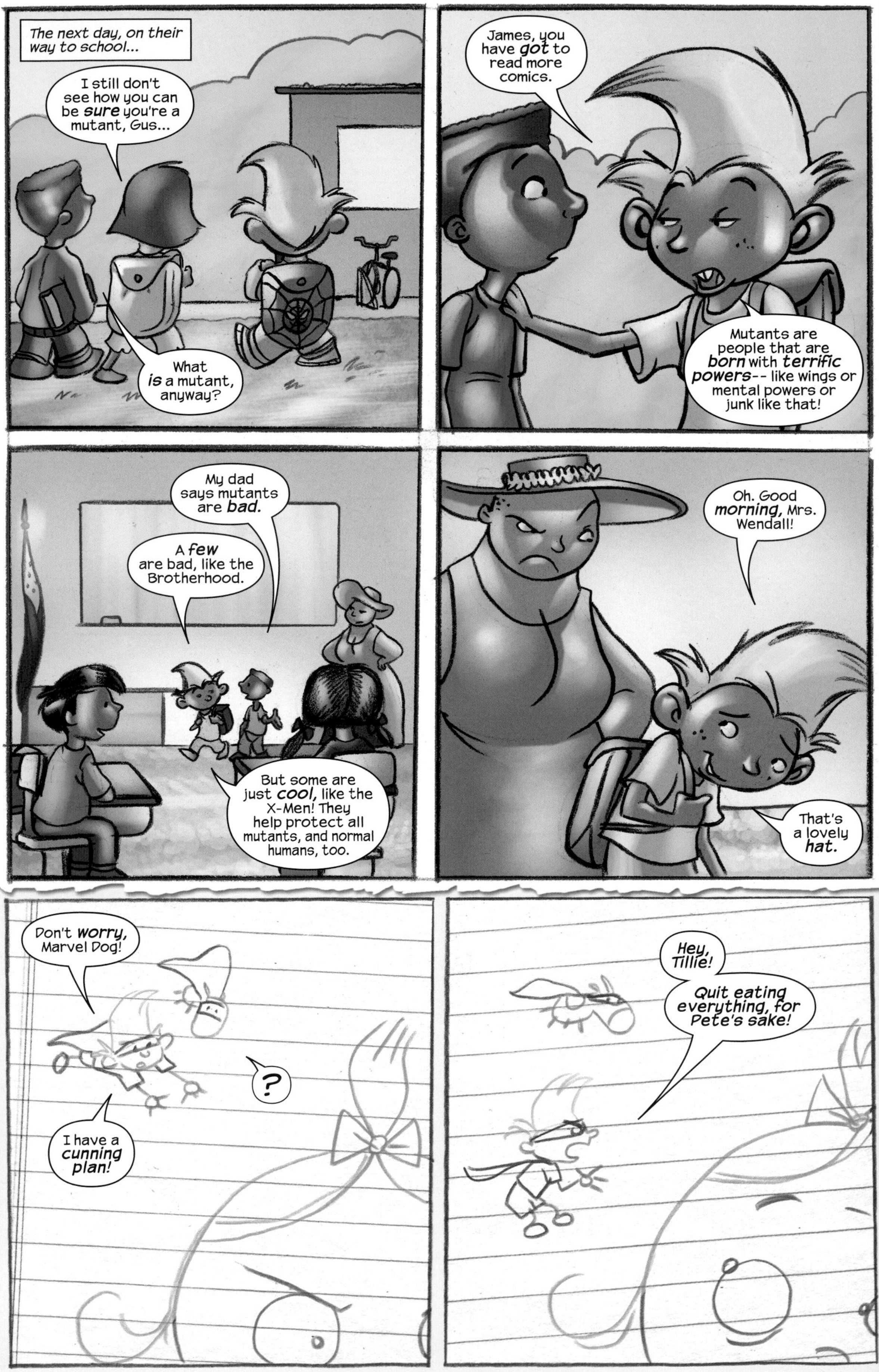
The next day, on their way to school...
I still don't see how you can be sure you're a mutant, Gus...
What is a mutant, anyway?
James, you have got to read more comics.
Mutants are people that are born with terrific powers-- like wings or mental powers or junk like that!
My dad says mutants are bad.
A few are bad, like the Brotherhood.
But some are just cool, like the X-Men! They help protect all mutants, and normal humans, too.
Oh. Good morning, Mrs. Wendall!
That's a lovely hat.
Don't worry, Marvel Dog!
?
I have a cunning plan!
Hey, Tillie!
Quit eating everything, for Pete's sake!

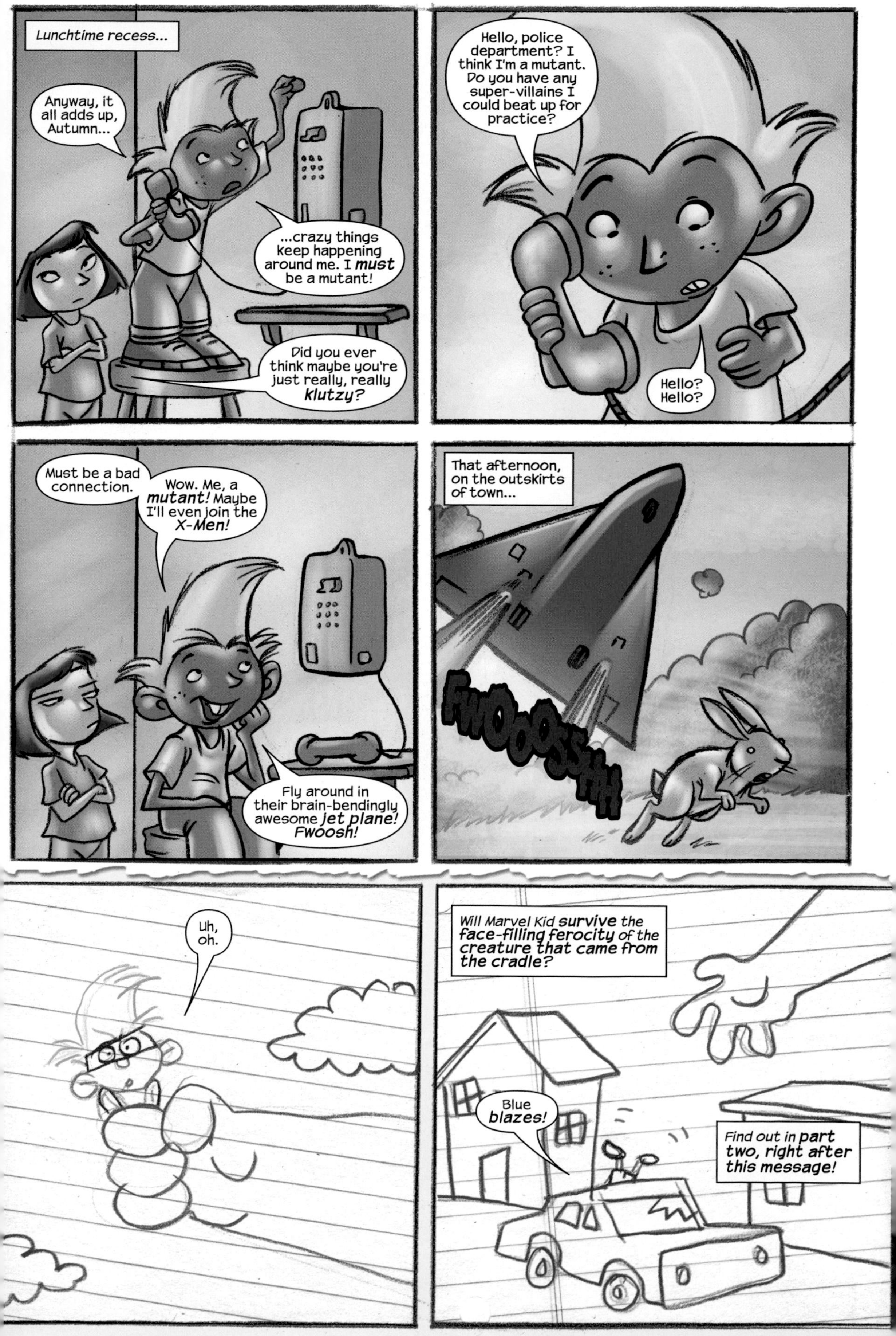
Lunchtime recess...
Anyway, it all adds up, Autumn...
...crazy things keep happening around me. I must be a mutant!
Did you ever think maybe you're just really, really klutzy?
Hello, police department? I think I'm a mutant. Do you have any super-villains I could beat up for practice?
Hello? Hello?
Must be a bad connection.
Wow. Me, a mutant! Maybe I'll even join the X-Men!
Fly around in their brain-bendingly awesome jet plane! Fwoosh!
That afternoon, on the outskirts of town...
FWOOOSSHH
Uh, oh.
Will Marvel Kid survive the face-filling ferocity of the creature that came from the cradle?
Blue blazes!
Find out in part two, right after this message!

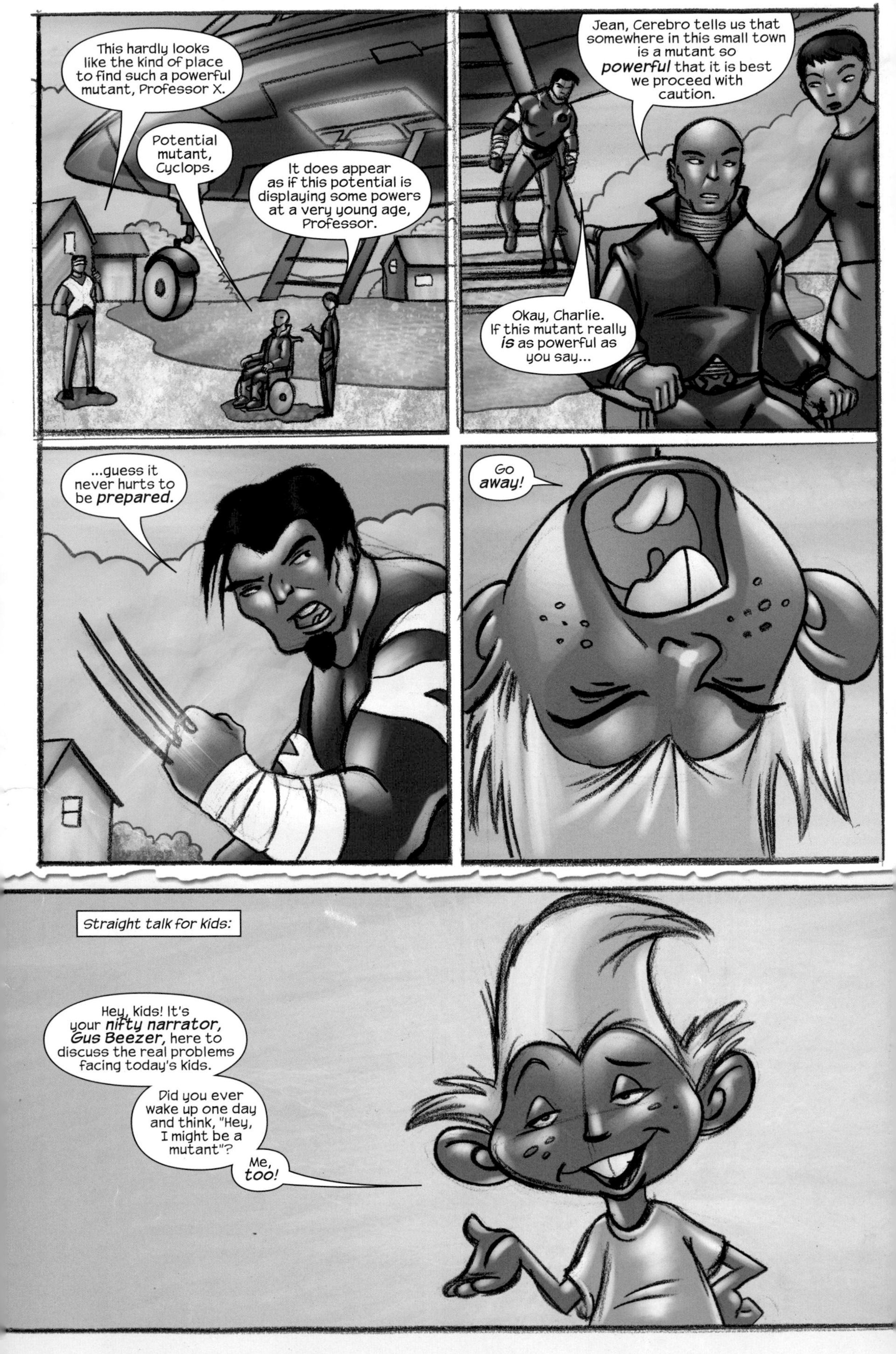
This hardly looks like the kind of place to find such a powerful mutant, Professor X.
Potential mutant, Cyclops.
It does appear as if this potential is displaying some powers at a very young age, Professor.
Jean, Cerebro tells us that somewhere in this small town is a mutant so powerful that it is best we proceed with caution.
Okay, Charlie. If this mutant really is as powerful as you say...
...guess it never hurts to be prepared.
Go away!
Straight talk for kids:
Hey, kids! It's your nifty narrator, Gus Beezer, here to discuss the real problems facing today's kids.
Did you ever wake up one day and think, "Hey, I might be a mutant"?
Me, too!

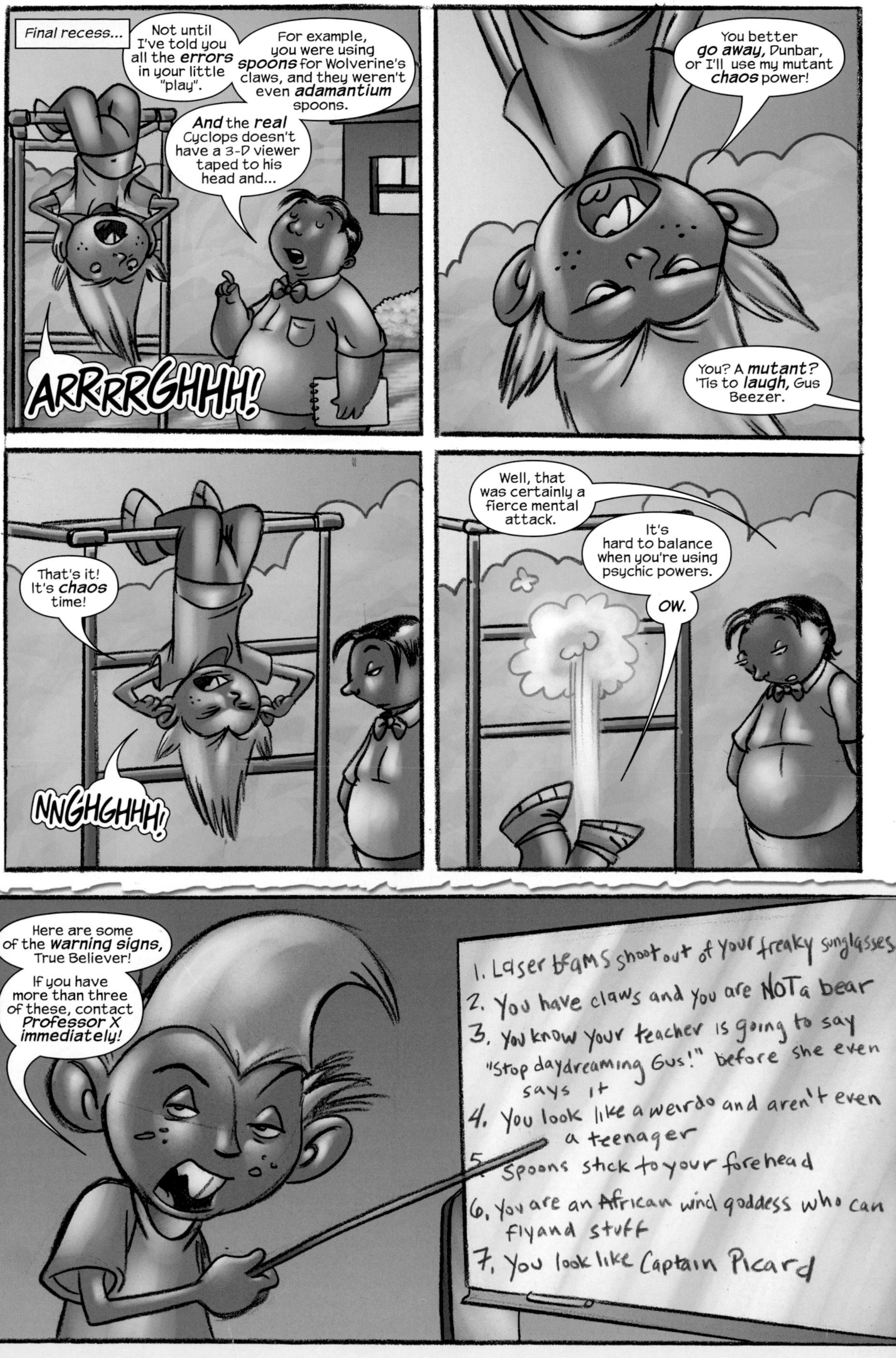
Final recess...
Not until I've told you all the errors in your little "play".
For example, you were using spoons for Wolverine's claws, and they weren't even adamantium spoons.
And the real Cyclops doesn't have a 3-D viewer taped to his head and...
ARRRRRGHHH!
You better go away, Dunbar, or I'll use my mutant chaos power!
You? A mutant? 'Tis to laugh, Gus Beezer.
That's it! It's chaos time!
NNGHGHHH!
Well, that was certainly a fierce mental attack.
It's hard to balance when you're using psychic powers.
OW.
Here are some of the warning signs, True Believer!
If you have more than three of these, contact Professor X immediately!
1. Laser beams shoot out of your freaky sunglasses
2. You have claws and you are NOT a bear
3. You know your teacher is going to say "Stop daydreaming Gus!" before she even says it
4. You look like a weirdo and aren't even a teenager
5. Spoons stick to your forehead
6. You are an African wind goddess who can fly and stuff
7. You look like Captain Picard

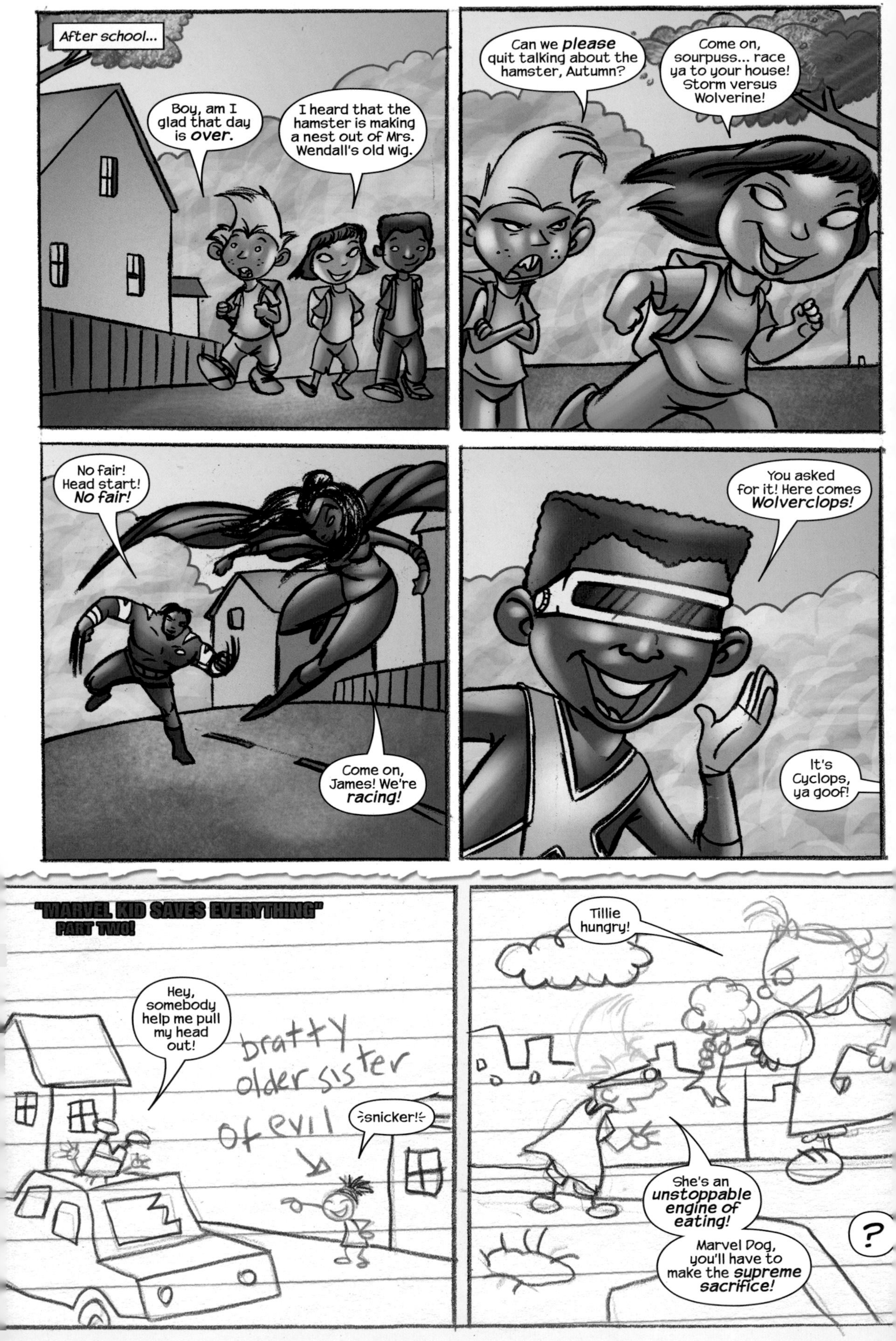
After school...
Boy, am I glad that day is *over.*
I heard that the hamster is making a nest out of Mrs. Wendall's old wig.
Can we *please* quit talking about the hamster, Autumn?
Come on, sourpuss... race ya to your house! Storm versus Wolverine!
No fair! Head start! *No fair!*
Come on, James! We're *racing!*
You asked for it! Here comes *Wolverclops!*
It's Cyclops, ya goof!
"MARVEL KID SAVES EVERYTHING" PART TWO!
Hey, somebody help me pull my head out!
bratty older sister of evil
snicker!
Tillie hungry!
She's an *unstoppable engine of eating!*
Marvel Dog, you'll have to make the *supreme sacrifice!*
?

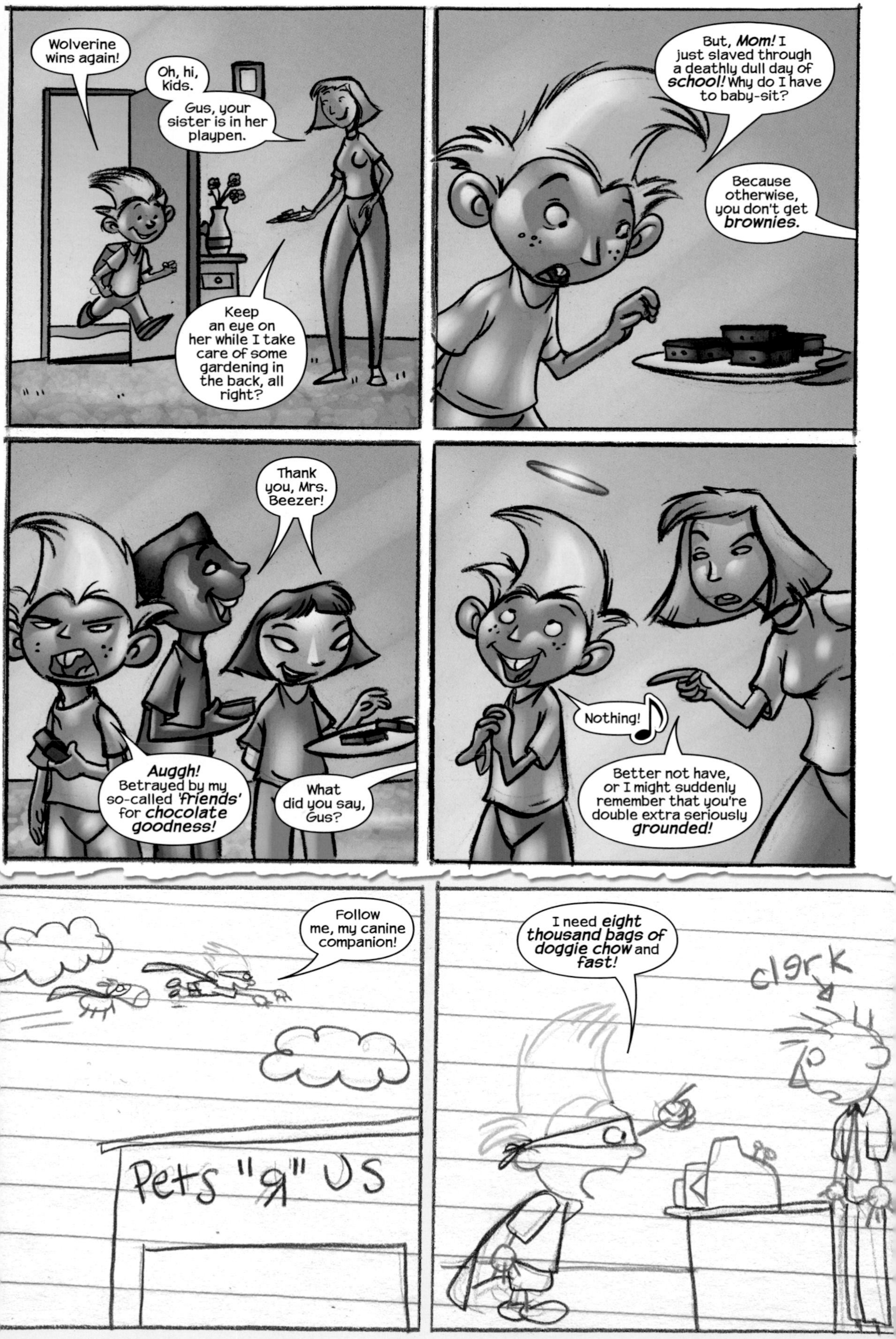
Wolverine wins again!
Oh, hi, kids.
Gus, your sister is in her playpen.
Keep an eye on her while I take care of some gardening in the back, all right?
But, Mom! I just slaved through a deathly dull day of school! Why do I have to baby-sit?
Because otherwise, you don't get brownies.
Thank you, Mrs. Beezer!
Auggh! Betrayed by my so-called 'friends' for chocolate goodness!
What did you say, Gus?
Nothing!
Better not have, or I might suddenly remember that you're double extra seriously grounded!
Follow me, my canine companion!
Pets "R" US
I need eight thousand bags of doggie chow and fast!
clerk

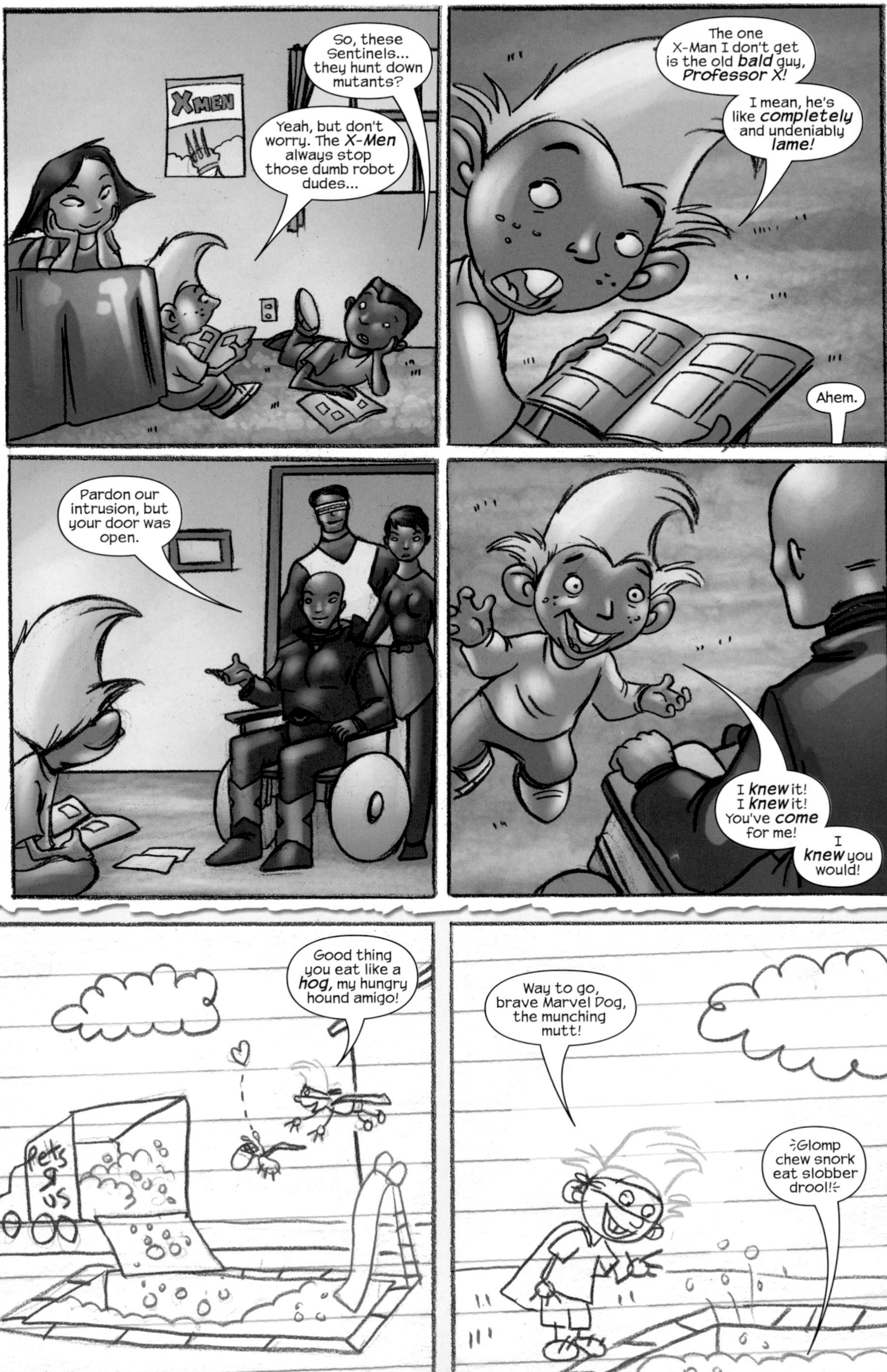

XMEN
So, these Sentinels... they hunt down mutants?
Yeah, but don't worry. The *X-Men* always stop those dumb robot dudes...
The one X-Man I don't get is the old **bald** guy, *Professor X!*
I mean, he's like ***completely*** and undeniably ***lame!***
Ahem.
Pardon our intrusion, but your door was open.
I ***knew*** it! I ***knew*** it! You've ***come*** for me!
I ***knew*** you would!
Good thing you eat like a ***hog,*** my hungry hound amigo!
Pets R US
Way to go, brave Marvel Dog, the munching mutt!
Glomp chew snork eat slobber drool!

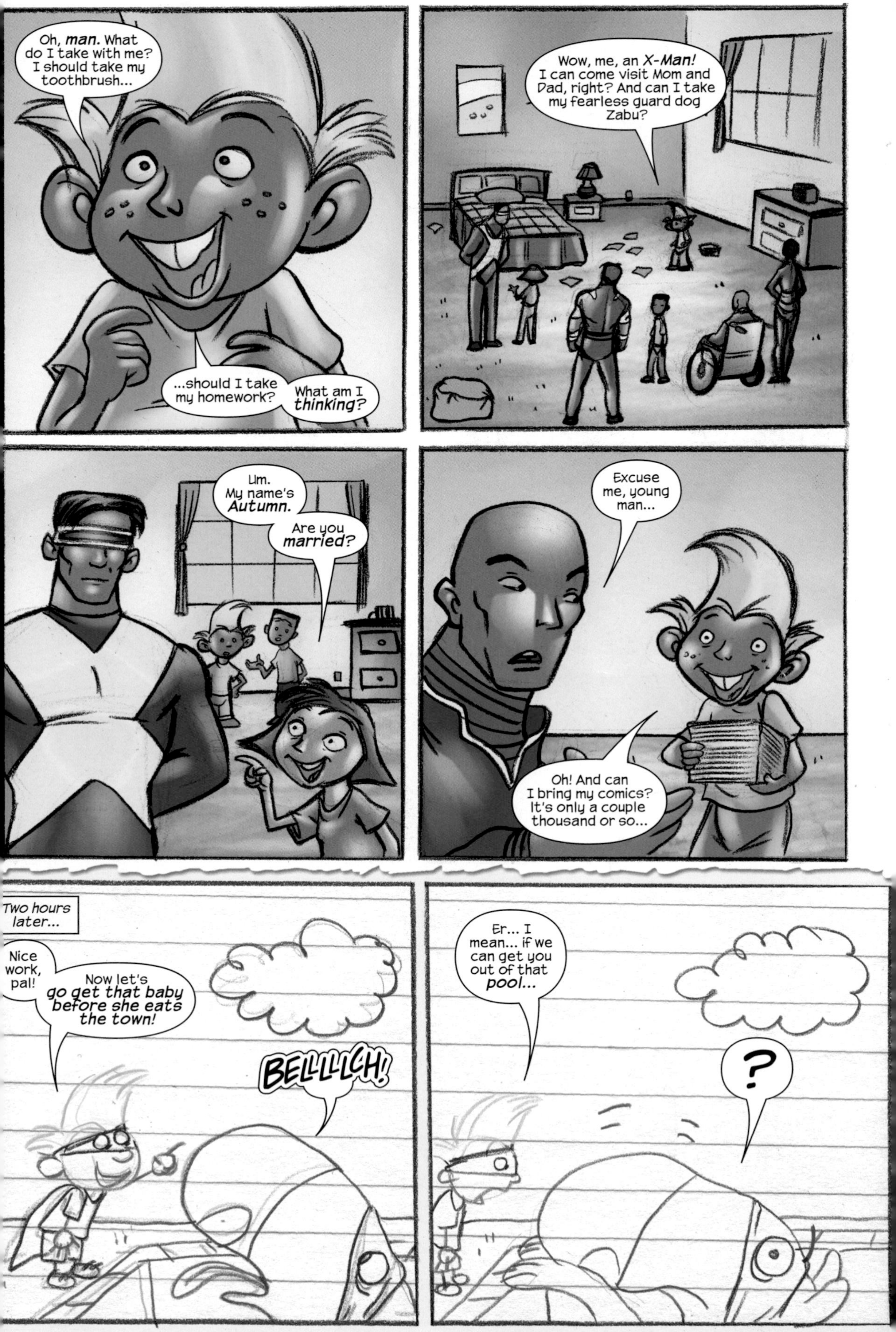
Oh, *man.* What do I take with me? I should take my toothbrush...
...should I take my homework?
What am I *thinking?*
Wow, me, an *X-Man!* I can come visit Mom and Dad, right? And can I take my fearless guard dog Zabu?
Um. My name's *Autumn.*
Are you *married?*
Excuse me, young man...
Oh! And can I bring my comics? It's only a couple thousand or so...
Two hours later...
Nice work, pal!
Now let's *go get that baby before she eats the town!*
BELLLLLCH!
Er... I mean... if we can get you out of that *pool...*
?

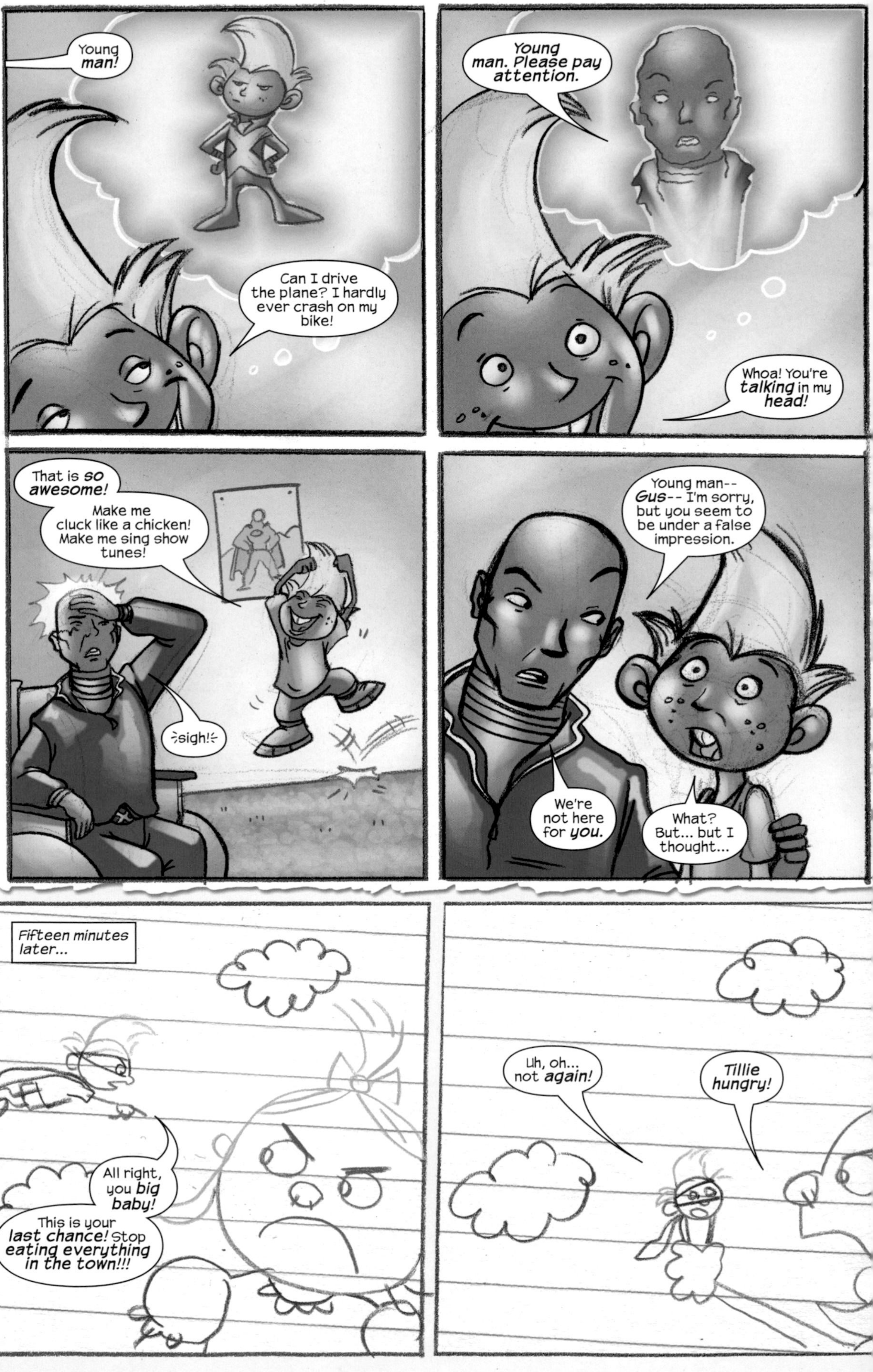
Young man!
Can I drive the plane? I hardly ever crash on my bike!
Young man. Please pay attention.
Whoa! You're talking in my head!
That is so awesome!
Make me cluck like a chicken! Make me sing show tunes!
sigh!
Young man-- Gus-- I'm sorry, but you seem to be under a false impression.
We're not here for you.
What? But... but I thought...
Fifteen minutes later...
All right, you big baby!
This is your last chance! Stop eating everything in the town!!!
Uh, oh... not again!
Tillie hungry!

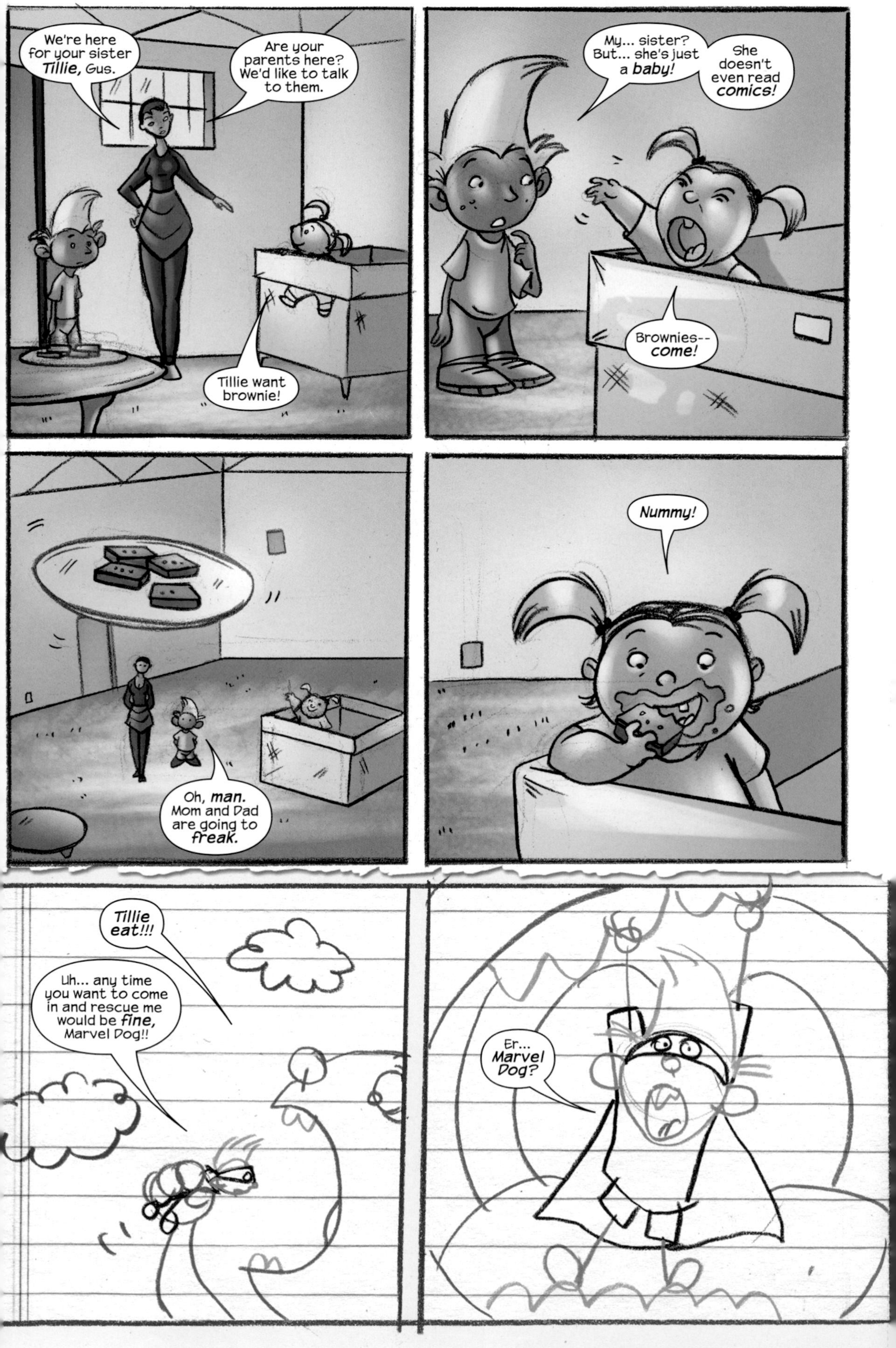
We're here for your sister *Tillie*, Gus.
Are your parents here? We'd like to talk to them.
Tillie want brownie!
My... sister? But... she's just a *baby!*
She doesn't even read *comics!*
Brownies-- *come!*
Oh, *man.* Mom and Dad are going to *freak.*
Nummy!
Tillie eat!!!
Uh... any time you want to come in and rescue me would be *fine,* Marvel Dog!!
Er... *Marvel Dog?*

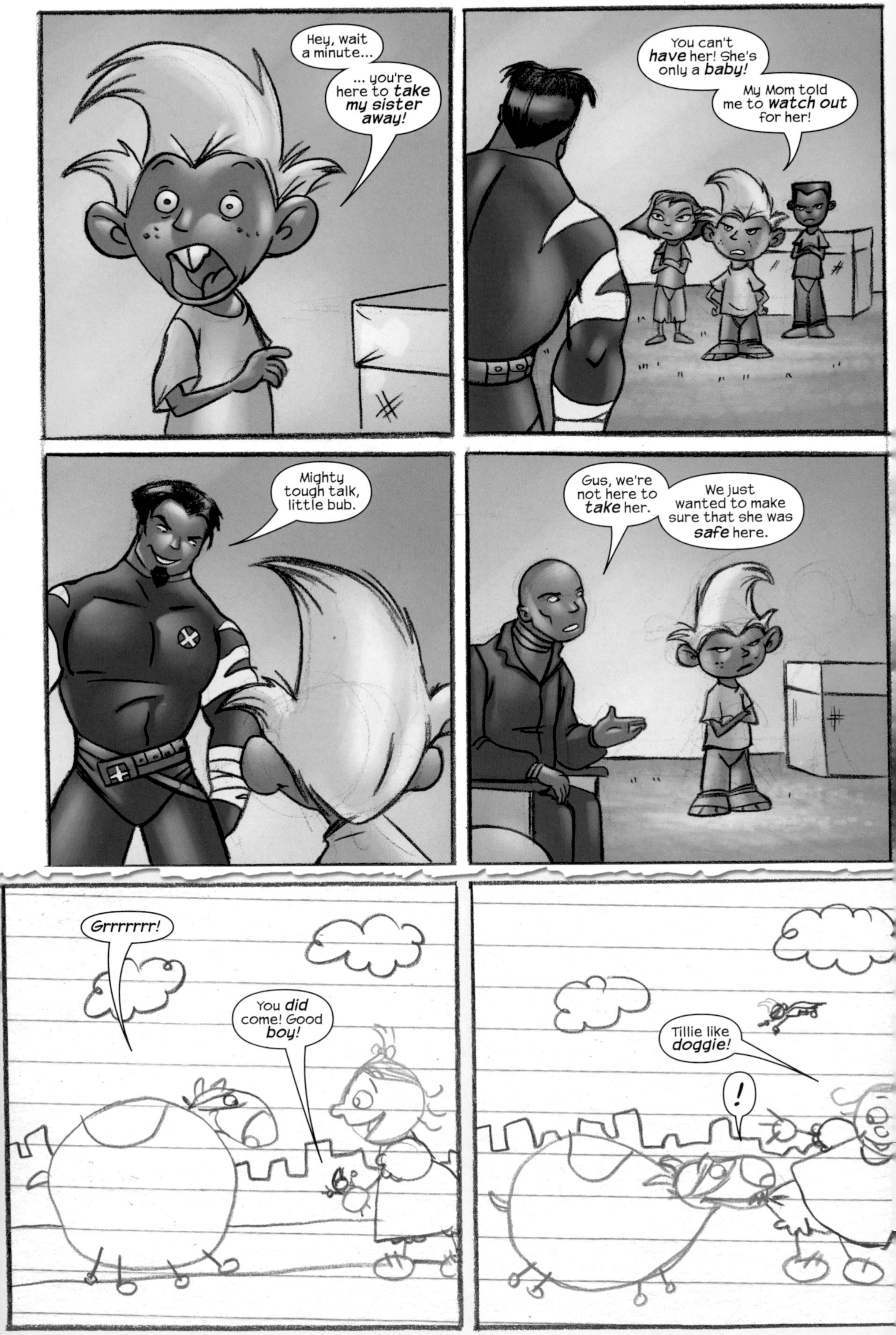
Hey, wait a minute...
... you're here to *take my sister away!*
You can't *have* her! She's only a *baby!*
My Mom told me to *watch out* for her!
Mighty tough talk, little bub.
Gus, we're not here to *take* her.
We just wanted to make sure that she was *safe* here.
Grrrrrrr!
You *did* come! Good *boy!*
Tillie like *doggie!*
!

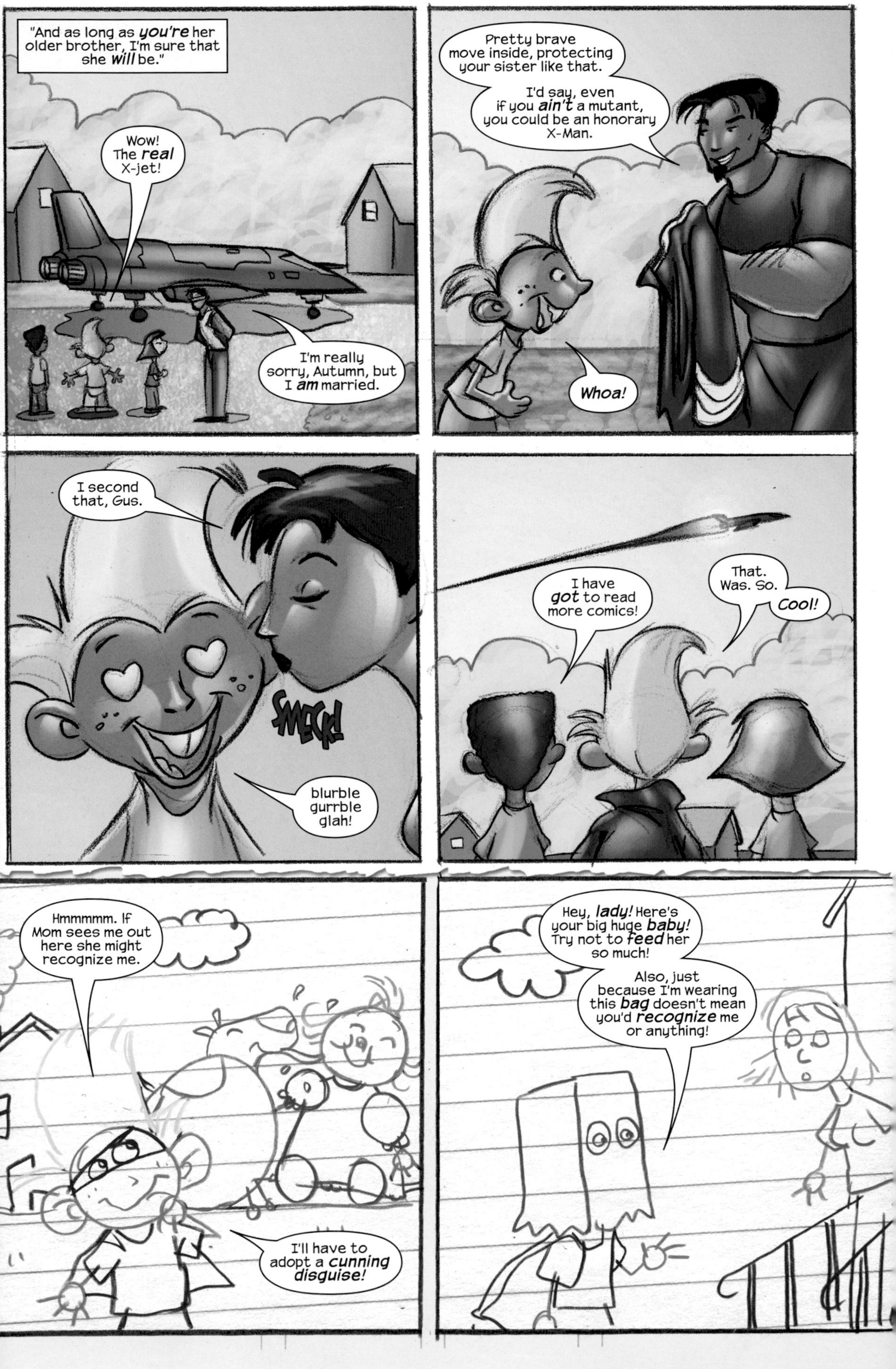
"And as long as *you're* her older brother, I'm sure that she *will* be."
Wow! The *real* X-jet!
I'm really sorry, Autumn, but I *am* married.
Pretty brave move inside, protecting your sister like that.
I'd say, even if you *ain't* a mutant, you could be an honorary X-Man.
Whoa!
I second that, Gus.
SMECK!
blurble gurrble glah!
I have *got* to read more comics!
That. Was. So. *Cool!*
Hmmmmm. If Mom sees me out here she might recognize me.
I'll have to adopt a *cunning disguise!*
Hey, *lady!* Here's your big huge *baby!* Try not to *feed* her so much!
Also, just because I'm wearing this *bag* doesn't mean you'd *recognize* me or anything!

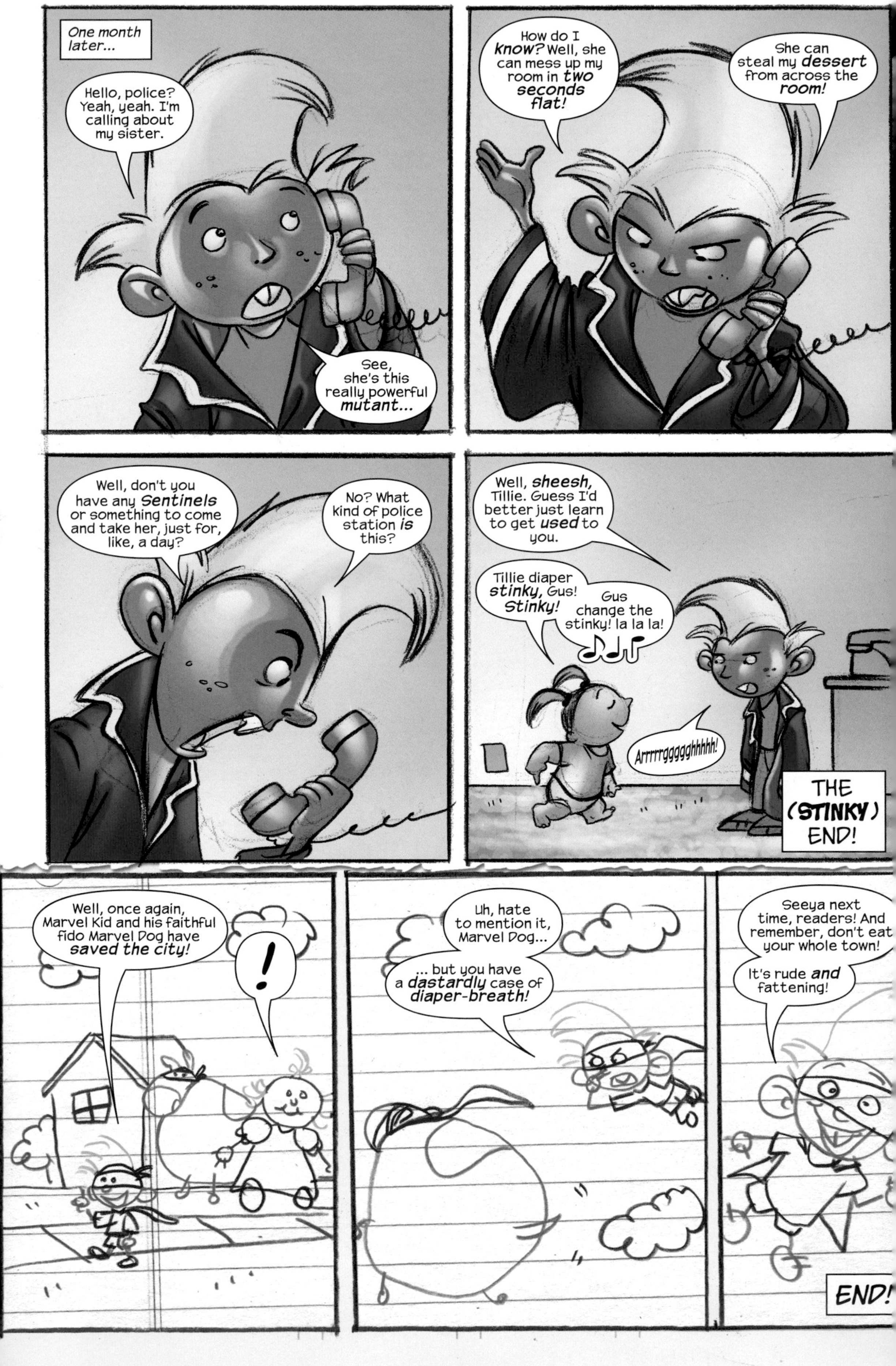
One month later...
Hello, police? Yeah, yeah. I'm calling about my sister.
See, she's this really powerful mutant...
How do I know? Well, she can mess up my room in two seconds flat!
She can steal my dessert from across the room!
Well, don't you have any Sentinels or something to come and take her, just for, like, a day?
No? What kind of police station is this?
Well, sheesh, Tillie. Guess I'd better just learn to get used to you.
Tillie diaper stinky, Gus! Stinky!
Gus change the stinky! la la la!
Arrrrrggggghhhhh!
THE (STINKY) END!
Well, once again, Marvel Kid and his faithful fido Marvel Dog have saved the city!
!
Uh, hate to mention it, Marvel Dog...
... but you have a dastardly case of diaper-breath!
Seeya next time, readers! And remember, don't eat your whole town!
It's rude and fattening!
END!